I0621524

THE SUPPER

*A complicated Love between a married Pastor
and a barely Catholic Christian.*

THE SUPPER

*A complicated Love between a married Pastor
and a barely Catholic Christian.*

Lydwine van Deinse

Copyright © 2018 — Lydwine van Deinse
All rights reserved.
First legal submission in France : December 2018
Self-publishing
ISBN: 9782956673422
Translated from French by Alexia Jacques Casanova

"They are inviting us to dinner, they want to meet you."

Blandina did not believe a word of what John had just said. She knew what awaited her: they wanted to judge and sentence her, for she was the tempting demon, just like Eve had tempted Adam, that poor idiot.

Keeping her thoughts to herself, she accepted the invitation with delight for she liked taking up challenges. Moreover, John had a lot of affection for this couple who had taken upon them to lead the stray sheep back to the fold. In clear terms, to give him back to his lawful wife.

Blandina was determined to please them, yet God knows she was starting with a serious disadvantage.

She took great care in getting ready.

She began by visiting her "beautician girlfriend." Makeup was an art she did not master and for her — no matter the subject — when in need, it was always better to speak to "those who know." Once home, Blandina picked her outfit. It was mid-May and the weather was very nice. She chose her most beautiful dress: a multicolored, finely knitted mesh, shining bright like a rainbow.

She pulled her hair up in a bun for a "good-girl" look and put on extra high-heeled sandals because she felt more confident when she was taller. She put on little jewelry, and decided not to smoke so she wouldn't have to take her bag. With John she did not need anything. Once ready, she gazed at herself in the mirror and felt satisfied.

But it was John who gave the final approval. When he came to pick her up, he found her so beautiful that he stared at her dumbfounded for a while.

"So? What is the matter with you?" she asked, "you look like you've just seen a ghost."

He smiled, pulled her against him, smelled her.

"An angel rather," he whispered.

They got into the car and left.

The encounter

First of all, it is important to underline that John's encounter with Blandina was made possible thanks to a chain of circumstances that began years earlier...

At that time, John thought he had lived everything, that he had examined each and every question from all sides and that nothing new or interesting could ever happen to him; and yet he was not so old. When he was only fifty, he had had a heart attack, and since then, having been very well insured, he had stopped working officially. He lived in a so-called "family" situation, which no longer made sense to him, but for reasons of comfort, tranquility and appearances, he continued as if "all was for the best in the best of all possible worlds. " John therefore believed with certainty that nothing nor anyone could come to disturb this quiet boredom. A very illusory and pretentious certainty indeed. But human beings are very pretentious, and this is probably the greatest evil of humanity. Locked up in their certainties, they can't see anything. They all know best than everybody else and spend their time trying to convince each other, willingly or forcibly, forgetting that there is no universal truth. But this is another story.

An unexpected meeting was slowly preparing in the shadows. The mechanisms that bring two people together are often extremely complex, like a puzzle of several thousand pieces. Parts form, separated from one other, little by little everything connects and finally the whole appears, bringing coherence to the existence of all these small pieces.

Blandina had been a neighbor of John's parents in her first year together with her ex-husband, 12 years ago. She did not know them very well, but on several occasions she had helped his mother carry her grocery bags and in doing so, had entered their house. She had spotted family photos on the living-room dresser, including one of John. She had asked his father, who was the man in the picture, "that's our son," he had answered, "not bad," she had said. John's father had laughed. Blandina could have met John at that time, but it did not happen and she and her husband moved out.

Life went on, as very chaotic for Blandina and ordered to the extreme for John, at least in appearance.

Years passed, John's mother fell ill, and in 2010 she died. John took his dad with him.

One day, as he was stepping out of his house with his father, he bumped into Blandina, who, recognizing John's father, greeted him warmly. She also greeted John, and asking for news, found out about his mother's death. She offered her condolences and then disappeared. John felt infatuated from the moment he met Blandina's gaze.

He asked a bunch of questions to his father who told him that Blandina had been their neighbor. John had but one thing on his mind: to see the woman who had brought such confusion within him. He had found her likeable, smiley, cheerful, full of life, but above all, irresistibly charming, with a primal sensuality that had echoed his, suddenly reminding him that he had one...

John was quick to discover what linked Blandina and the couple with a little girl who had just moved into the house next door. The woman was none other than Blandina's best friend! From that day, John did everything to get in touch with her.

One evening that he was watching out for her, he walked out and up to her as soon as he saw her on the pretext of wanting to thank her for the services rendered to his mother. Blandina graciously received his thanks, but then, just like she had the first time they had met, she disappeared.

Each time, the need to see her again was becoming stronger and he would go out of his way to come up with ploys that would get him to be in contact with her.

Another night, he took advantage of the fact that Blandina's car — who would always park badly — was likely to block the way, and went to knock on his neighbors' door. Blandina was about to leave. She was dressed in black and, seeing her, he felt his heart beat faster; he already wanted her.

"I'm sorry, your car needs to be moved…"

"I'm leaving, I'm leaving, sorry," she said laughing.

John slowly started to leave and as soon as he felt Blandina walking behind him, he turned around, came back to face her and said:

"I forgot to say good night," and he nervously kissed her on the cheeks.

Soon enough, almost every time Blandina came to visit her friend, John managed to run into her, greet her with a kiss on the cheek, chat and joke with her a little. He enjoyed more and more being in her presence and getting close to her was becoming a necessity for him.

One day, as her car was particularly badly parked, with hazard lights on, John seized the opportunity to ask her, once again, to move her vehicle. She offered him her car keys so he could do it himself.

"I'm not used to automatic cars; I don't know if I can do it."

Blandina looked at him incredulously.

"Are you dumb or something? Come on, I'll show you."

She had a slight, mocking smile which, added to her remark, finished to destabilize him. He did what everyone does in these cases: he giggled nervously.

John sat in the car and Blandina slid her bust over his to engage the gearbox, their bodies touched through their clothes…

They had never been so close.

John smelled her perfume, felt her body against his, and then he could not feel anything else. He felt like he had no air left to breathe as if she had taken everything, he knew at that moment that he loved her … that he had fallen madly in love with her!

As for Blandina, she was running into the Pastor from time to time since her best friend had moved in the house next to his and he always showed her a lot of sympathy in greeting her, but she was far from imagining what awaited her...

The declaration

One day when she was driving in the rain, she saw him on the side of the road beckoning her to stop, he wanted to talk to her. She therefore invited him to get in the car to shelter from the rain, without thinking twice about what he might have to say.

Some moments of our lives are taken care of directly by our souls. These are moments of great serenity where one acts without hesitation and without thinking, but without precipitation either. In hindsight, when we describe those moments that we do not understand, we can still say: "It was the most natural thing in the world." And that's exactly how Blandina had acted. She had invited the Pastor to get in the car in "the most natural way." And it was also in "the most natural way" that he had declared his Love to her...

Seated, his body turned towards her, looking into her eyes, without hesitating, he entirely opened up to her. It was romantic, light and spiritual at the same time. She had never heard a more moving statement.

She was touched, right in the heart.

But although she received his confession as one receives a gift, with much pleasure, she told him that her heart was already taken. She was in a relationship.

He did not seem to hear...

As soon as he left, she began to ponder... Holding the business card he had given her, she wondered: why was she so touched, so charmed by this declaration? Why was she following up on it?

His name was John. He was a Protestant pastor. He was a construction expert. He was married. He painted too. Besides that, he had told her a lot about him, probably all she needed to know, as everyone does in a first conversation when they really want to start something.

Unfortunately, one rarely remembers everything from this precious first conversation, and it is a pity, for in general, absolutely everything is there, chaotically presented, still everything is there. So he had told her about his seemingly orderly, uneventful life, where everything appeared absolutely under control, even his extramarital affairs. Yes, although he was Pastor, he was a man like so many others. She had immediately perceived a devastating and morbid emotional void. No wonder he had had a heart attack! His heart, tired of beating for nothing, had almost stopped for good.

Blandina was not long in realizing that she was completely capsized by this declaration of Love and that same evening, she wrote him this email:

If I tell you that all my certainties have been shattered, that I thought I knew everything about Love, but that I was wrong, that I thought we chose Love when it is Love which chooses us and that the only freedom we have is to follow or to flee it.

You spoke to me about Love, and the echo it provoked resounds throughout my being.

I would like to tell you stories about me, but they seem so futile. Slices of an idiotic and useless life. Me, who thought I was destined for an exceptional fate, at 43 I don't have children and everything seems to indicate that I never will, then, what is the meaning of this life, what is my role?

I can still hear you talking to me and I tell myself that I'm lucky to have met you, even if it terrorizes me. I know that the great geometer of the universe has very precise measurements that leave no room for chance, and that he is fundamentally good for us, and that in order to understand him one must be very patient, but here, you see, I'm feeling lost. I naively thought I could impose an iron-like emotional discipline on myself, and someone rightly pointed out to me that even iron bends when heated...

I can tell you that I smoke and drink too much and that it plays tricks on me.

That I always eat too much chocolate to the point of making me sick, but that I do it again and again.

That the times when I truly feel good are the ones I spend alone because I am easily influenced and I hate it. I can tell you that I am passionate about classical music, but that there are very few people around me who share this passion and that I am therefore deprived of it.

That you touched me, directly, right in the heart…

I do not know if I will have the courage to live what is planned for me. Everything you have told me has been living in my dreams for as long as I can remember.

An immense weariness invades me…

He had told her about Love like Glenn Gould plays a Bach concerto, and as with music, she had been overwhelmed by everything he had told her. She had heard a wonderful tale, and the storyteller had chosen her, to listen to it. She felt ready to give anything as long as he kept telling the tale…

She had just fallen in love.

"Could we be lovers?" It seemed impossible to her, and yet it was distressingly banal.

"Love is very patient," he had said…

Then he would have to wait patiently. By writing to him on that very evening, Blandine was following up on his declaration.

The follow-up

They started exchanging letters regularly, each one more passionate than the last. Then came phone calls, growing longer every time. Finally, she accepted a date — a quick one, on the sly — then another date, again quick and concealed, then a kiss…

But quickly, the fear of being discovered prevailed.

If she had been certain that her relationship with John could never be discovered, she would have thrown herself into it without restraint; but the fact is, there was no such certainty.

How many of her friends — male and female — had been caught in adultery, when they were convinced it could never happen to them? And, even if from the outside these stories could make one smile, or even laugh, from the inside, they would always cause drama. How was it possible that something as banal as adultery, which generously fed literature, theater, cinema, often in the form of comedy, could plunge its protagonists into despair? Blandina could not answer that question, she could only observe what was happening. And she did not wish for herself to become the heroine of a tragedy. So very quickly, her stress levels reached beyond what she could bear.

There had been this short rendezvous in her car, during which she had not stopped checking that her mobile phone was off until she decided to remove the battery for more safety. But even after she did so, every car, every pedestrian — there only had been a couple of them — terrorized her. It was past seven, one night in January, it had been dark out for a long time, they were in a completely isolated place and yet, this did not make a difference, she was freaking out. They had talked a good half hour, and it was there that she had taken the liberty and the risk to kiss him, just once… She had liked it, yes, really liked it, more than "liked" actually, since this kiss wouldn't stop spreading its magic…

When they had parted, all the windows of the car were fogged, and she had had to drive with her windows open despite the cold to make it go away. A little stressed, but so enchanted. She had kissed him, convinced that she would hate it, and that it would all stop there; but far from hating it, and much more than an enchantment, she had let herself be bewitched by this kiss.

He had nevertheless offered to stop sending her messages and emails if it could bring her relief. The deep sigh she let out in response to his proposal expressed all her gratitude. She could leave her phone unattended again.

Blandina could not see clearly, and for good reason, it was all so sudden. However, she asked him to meet her a day or two later on a beach, once again in the early evening, when it was already dark.

When he arrived he embraced her affectionately, but she gently pushed him away, because here again, she felt surrounded by spies. There were joggers and she feared that one of them would know her.

They talked a lot, they laughed too, but she felt that she was intimidating him. She told him about it and he recognized it. She knew she sometimes made a strong impression on men. In addition to being beautiful and desirable, one of her friends had told her that she had such a sense of freedom, that she could seem elusive, as immaterial as a dream. And so these men did not dare to touch her for fear that she would disappear.

That evening, they parted with the implicit and illusory promise to meet again very quickly, under the same conditions.

But she had overestimated her ability to manage stress.

The next day, he requested a similar meeting which she refused. She no longer allowed him to ask for some of her time. From there, she declined or cancelled almost systematically all the rendezvous he was asking for. It was she who decided where and when and even if, they could see each other.

She wanted to confide in her friend Robert about this affair, whom, having mastered the art of adultery, would listen closely and, hopefully, give her good advice.

He invited her to lunch and they spoke passionately for more than three hours.

He told her his story, and gave him his reasons... He listened to hers and helped her figure things out.

What did she really want? What was she missing?

From what she had said, he had deduced that this man who claimed to be "so enamored of her " would not be satisfied with just a casual fuck. The proof was that he had let her kiss him without going further. "If it had been me, I guarantee you that I would touched you so intensely everywhere that you would have been mad with desire and before you even know it, you would have left, with a smile on your lips and your panties in one hand!"

She had burst out in laughter. Of course, from this perspective adultery was seductive. She had had a great time with him, but throughout lunch, she could not stop checking her phone and the people at the tables nearby. She decided at the end of the meal that she had to put this relationship on hold, before it went further. This constant anxiety, this paranoia, these worries about her cellphone or her email inbox, it was all too much for her right now. She was in a period of doubt, of course, but that did not mean she no longer loved the man she was sharing her life with. She told herself that if she wanted to take stock of the situation, she had to evade all influence. If she made the decision to leave her partner, it would be because she did not love him anymore, not because she had fell for another man.

First break-up

She called John, but it seems like she didn't speak clearly since he understood that their story was ending there.

He talked about being sidelined, about being disposed of, about the "blow of axe" he had just been struck with. Anyway, it was a disaster. She instantly congratulated herself for nipping this story in the bud. She did not even dare to imagine what would have happened if...

Blandina, having heard his dismay, still took the trouble to write to him:

What was I supposed to do? I asked you for some time to reflect, and you heard well: it's over, there's nothing left.

How did you not notice the tremendous stress that our short meetings gave me? How did you not notice that I would check 25 times if my phone was off, that I was seeing spies everywhere, that even at home, when calling you, I was afraid I might not be alone and that someone could hear me talking to you. If I do not love him anymore, I leave him, if I love him I stop seeing you, but I can't continue this not so innocent game. For you there is nothing wrong in what we are doing, but imagine that I were with you and doing this with another man... How would this make you feel if you found out?

If I have a decision to make, I will do so independently of you. I will not put the blame on you for the choices I make. And if you love me, you will love me the same in six months or in a year. I am not worried. It was good to be with you, but it was taking too much from me.

He claimed to be deeply in love with her. He had said that Love was very patient. She had listened and loved his words. So, if Love was patient, she had plenty of time to make her decision. And that's precisely what she intended to do — to take her time. Making rushed decision had not proved successful until then.

For the time being, she needed peace.

However, it wasn't impossible that she would feel the urge to talk to him — maybe even see him — the next day. She vowed to resist this urge.

To hold on at least... How much time should she allow herself before giving in?

She felt immensely relieved to have cut off all communication. She was thinking of him, of course, and she even had the temptation to get in touch with him, but she quickly remembered the unbearable discomfort she felt every time they had seen or even called each other. If they loved each other, if they were made for each other, there was no reason to rush things.

She decided to give all of herself to Stephen, her official darling, to find out whether or not she still loved him. She had an infinite tenderness for him, but was it Love? For some time now, she had lost the desire to make love with him, she no longer felt arousal and it would hurt when he penetrated her. John had awakened the sexual animal within her, and even if she had not made Love with him, this arousal... it felt good.

It therefore turned out impossible for her to wipe John from her mind, and despite her good resolutions, Blandina secretly hoped that John would call her back, for she was missing him.

She would devise a thousand scenarios. She would fantasize, from morning to night that she was meeting him unexpectedly and stealing a kiss from him. She imagined him burning with desire for her, secretly observing her when she visited her friend, his neighbor. In the morning, she would get ready, thinking of him. She believed in the possibility of bumping into him and it made her happy. And on the rare occasions she made love, she was thinking of him.

In the evening, she would fall asleep in the arms of Morpheus, who, versed in the art of taking any human form, turned into John. And so she could see him, touch him, kiss him...

Resumption

For days and days, he remained without giving her any news, then one morning, finally, he sent her a message inviting her for coffee. "With pleasure!" she immediately replied, and smiling to her ears, she met him at his place. It goes without saying that his wife was away. He was disarmed by her smile which he took as a sign of amusement on her part, but in reality, it was a smile of happiness, Blandina was delighted to see him again.

He told her his yearnings, his doubts, his questions, a little bit of his grief, but she could only gaze at him, without fully listening. When he was speaking seriously, he had a way of crossing his arms over his chest, which she adored. He seemed to be trying to stress his words with this gesture. He did it again and again, and she relished observing this movement which she found absolutely perfect. She spent a bit more than a half-hour with him. When they said goodbye, the urge to kiss him felt so strong that she was surprised not to yield to it. Long after, she was still thinking about it, and the desire remained intact, and that feeling, it was good. She was replaying that goodbye scene over and over in her mind; that moment when their faces were getting closer, and she could still feel the strong current attracting her to him like a magnet.

She thought, "if you make Love like you kiss me, Lord have mercy on me …"

More drama, more emails

A few days passed during which they exchanged some emails and text messages. She had an obsessive fear of being discovered, but she suddenly felt so alive. She would reply in full and was delighted to read him. He thought she would consent to go further, so when he offered her to meet at the hotel he did not understand her refusal.

He had been in love with her so completely and for so many weeks, that he had forgotten that he had only recently declared his flame. For weeks and weeks he had watched her, multiplied the opportunities to greet her, to talk to her, to cross her way, to smell her ... And she smelled so good.

Not only did he not understand his refusal, he did not accept it either. Everything was confused in his head.

He said he did not want any more news from her, and then he said that he was suffering from not receiving any.

He said he would take what comes, then he said he preferred to have nothing if he could not have everything.

He said ... everything and its opposite. Once again, it was a disaster.

She wondered how he got to this point in such a short time.

As if, trying to light a candle, she had set the whole house on fire. Of course, she believed him to be sincere, but his reactions were not justified, even less simple or light, the two major qualities which she ascribed to Love. She was upset to see him suffering, but he was not suffering because of her, of that she was intimately convinced. She had listened to his story and he had revealed, from their first conversations, just about everything that explained his present suffering. No, he was not suffering because of her, he was suffering from not having loved for so long; maybe from not having ever loved. He was suffering from seeing all this lost time, he was suffering from having deluded himself with material satisfactions. If material satisfactions could fill the heart, rich people would never commit suicide. He was suffering from having believed he was safe, in his beautiful scenery where everything was tidy, in its place, where nothing spilled, while the poison was inside.

We can ignore and silence our emotions, but we can not make them disappear, for they are there, and they always find a way out, much slower than tears, but infinitely more painful.

He had turned a blind eye on his need to love, to love passionately. He began with a heart attack, which effectively stopped him in his progression to nothingness. It would have been time to sit down and reflect. But he most likely ignored that message. So, inevitably, when a few years later, Blandina appeared in his life, instead of just falling in love, and feeling like he could fly by just thinking of her, like all true lovers who feel invulnerable, lovers to whom everything seems easy, instead of this happiness, his heart exploded a second time and it was extremely painful.

Although Love fills, he felt empty. If, at the first warning, he had stopped to think, if he had made the effort to understand that he was wrong and that he had been wrong for years, he would have known how to continue to lead the Good Fight the one we fight in the name of our dreams[1], and the serenity, indispensable to all lightness, would have been restored to him. But his dreams, ignored, buried, and scorned for so long may have ended up dying... If that was the case, his suffering was far from over.

She felt for him, his confession had touched her, his distress too, but if he didn't resolve to assess the extent of the damage and start fixing it, she could not do it for him. And after all, he was an "expert", evaluating was his job, he had dedicated most of his life to evaluations, so he had both the knowledge and ability to do it.

Nevertheless, Blandina, listening only to her heart and although he had asked her not to contact him, decided to write him anyway, just like that ...

---
1   Paulo Coelho, The Pilgrimage (1987)

I'm writing to you; this way it almost feels like I'm with you. You are in no way obliged to read me.

I think I understand you a little, but only a little. I know you have been sincere from the beginning, only you overestimated what you could accept. I would not have accepted a fraction of it, except that I would never have solicited a married man. Anyway! We can't change the beginning of our story, and it would be a shame to, because it was very good.

Maybe not having access to you as easily as I could, will force me to ask myself the right questions. What happens when you get close to me does not help me think. And I wonder, is it just a physical thing?

I know that I was insensitive, that I certainly hurt you and I beg your pardon. But those stolen moments with you have filled me with warmth, sweetness, well-being, and I play them on repeat in my mind, like children watch the same cartoon over and over again. These moments are like instants of eternity, timeless and permanent. I relive them every time I think about it, like a dream that could be directed. And then, I imagine the scene where we meet again, and that one I adore because it is powerful.

I wanted to tell you that since you came around I feel beautiful again, and also, I feel so alive, and also, do not believe that my lovers have adored and idolized me. Anyway, it doesn't matter, what is important, you see, it's the good that you did to me. If my certainties were shattered, it is because they weren't so solid.

I do not aspire to a quiet existence, especially since I have no children, I can risk everything. I feel like a groundhog just out of hibernation.

You reminded me what it meant to be alive, carnally, it's so good, but not only. So, let's go back to our first break-up, when I told you that I was not worried, that's true, and I have a decision to make, which is independent of you. You see, I don't change my mind so easily. At the very beginning, you sent me a text message (one among many others) in which you wrote "we are made for each other" and I replied "in another life."

This other life starts when I decide to change the current one.

I kiss you like I did on Tuesday, and I run my fingers through your hair, while I find the courage to live what is planned for me. And also, if my writing bothers you, let me know, I'll try not to do it anymore. But I love writing to you, so if I can no longer see you, talk to you, or even write to you, I may fade for good.

Needless to say that after this email, it was he who was hit straight in the heart. And although he said he no longer wanted to be in touch, he replied that very evening.

Good evening darling, it is 9:43 pm, I have read your email several times. First of all, I will always read your emails whatever happens, and I will also be waiting for your texts and calls. As a matter of fact, I spent the entire day checking my phone for a call or text from you. Today, Cupid hit me again, and believe me, the pain is as much physical as it is in my soul. I have been unfair, pretentious, mean and above all arrogant; and it all came back around to me like a boomerang in the face. You're right I overestimated my ability to manage everything, but my Love for you and the need for your presence were stronger. I long to see you happy; not hurt you or make you feel bad. I have failed and I beg your pardon! Today I don't know how to act anymore, but what I'm sure of is that for me you are a necessity, a vital necessity, I can no longer be nor think of a future without you! In your email, you told me very nice things, it confused and disarmed me even more! Is it important for you to now whether it is only a physical thing? I do not know how you can figure this out, but be assured that it is more than just physical for me. What to do, what should we do? I considered leaving for a few days, to get away from you, but you would have been in everywhere in my thoughts and I would have just moved away from you physically.

Last night, I wanted to drink and forget, but I changed my mind.

Drinking was not the answer, but drinking could make the question go away. And then I feared the painful awakening. As I told you, I was ready to leave everything behind if I had to, to live on Love alone and in sandals as long as I'm with you!

I don't know what's next, what you will decide or what we will decide. What I do know is that I suffer without you, that I need you and that I love you.

Be assured that I will always be waiting for your calls, texts and emails!

I'll stop here for tonight, I still have things to tell you, but it's an inexhaustible source. I adore and love your kisses! I do not want you to fade, you're beautiful and you attract me! Since last night, we haven't stopped talking without seeing each other and see where I'm at. This is one of the reasons I regretfully refused to have coffee with you, because I knew what the consequences could be.

All of this happened years ago … There had been emails, hundreds of them, and quick rendezvous, in a hurry, impassioned hugs and kisses, but neither one nor the other were single when they had met. And if fate hadn't interfered, it is likely that they would have remained as such. He had desired her so, that he was still burning just thinking about it.

Having only their email exchanges, for their meetings were so brief and rare, and re-reading them constantly, he had come to know them by heart, and even today he could recite them word for word.

To avoid being discovered, they had each created an email address that only them knew of and which they used exclusively for their passionate exchanges.

John — continually frustrated, hurt, sometimes desperate not to possess her — accumulated blunders and faux-pas, and they argued a great deal, broke up on the web, then made up again. She was perpetually hesitant, taking two steps back for each step towards him.

Valentine's Day and then

He remembered Valentine's Day, lovers' day, he had got a bouquet of red roses delivered to her, and she, had pretended to believe that it was Stephen, her spouse, who had offered them. When the latter had objected that the flowers weren't from him, she had cleverly turned the situation into blame! How come those roses weren't from him? Avoiding the real question: "Who offered you the roses? "

This day, however, was not a success. He had written a long email to her.

Monday, February 14, 2011

Hello,

My first thoughts of the day begin with you! Tradition has it that on this day we celebrate Lovers! What can we wish for, or do? Logically, in most cases, lovers get to be together and celebrate from 1 am until midnight; their Love is effusive, with presence, attention, affection, etc. And this should end with a relationship in which both bodies come into one! It's paradoxical for I do not know when I will get a chance to have you near me, and it would only be for a fleeting moment. Besides, I won't get to share what the majority of couples will experience on this day, and it is with another man that you will end up today! Maybe the adage about the flip side of the coin based on things from the past is now becoming a reality? To be honest with you, I did not think I would ever experience this kind of situation. I have very rarely been in the position of a lover who does not have control or decide of the times and moments spent with his beloved!

This is the first time in my life — of course there's a first time for everything — that I am in a romantic or sentimental relationship of this kind. It is almost an impossible Love, even a destructive one where everything seems to be against us! As you say, I'm married, full of habits, you're not single, still in love. It seems that he told you recently that he was still in love with you. Your fears of failure and of what people might say, your life which, despite what you think, appears also very tidy, all these things seem insurmountable obstacles.

Yesterday evening, I stumbled upon a TV show called "Giving it all up for Love" I watched only one story, for there were several of them. It was a woman and a man who were both married, and who meet again after several years. They had been in love at some point in their lives. She lived in an exotic country in the sun and had a daughter. They accidentally re-connect through internet, exchange a lot of emails, become dependent on these exchanges until the day he writes her to say that he had never stopped loving her, that he had never forgotten her. As it was mutual, they each left their respective spouse without hesitating, got together, got married and had a little baby! They are very happy and they have no regret whatsoever, and yet she left her idyllic environment behind and they now live in the north, I think, somewhere in the countryside.

What makes us undecided? Maybe Love is not as strong as it seems?

I often feel like running away from you, putting an end to our relationship. It's not that I'm afraid of failure, but often you intrigue me, I struggle to really discern your deep thoughts, your desires, your way of dealing with Love and all its contradictions, in fact I do not know where it's going, instead of seeing the end of the tunnel I feel like I'm entering it without the certainty that there will be light again. I do not think I'm short of patience, of course when I'm with you I don't want it to end, the opposite would be abnormal! I find that you have a disconcerting ease to move on, certainly you must be in the truth and certainly it saves you a lot of useless pain or suffering! Unlike what you think, my position is not comfortable at all, your most intimate moments are not for me, even if your situation was already like that when I declared my love to you.

That being said, this day should not be about analyses or contradictions, let's keep it simple and the time we spend together on this day will always be better than nothing! It's your day, my day, may it be beautiful and wonderful for both of us!

Too frustrated not to spend this whole "lovers' day" with her, he was bitter and had preferred not to see her at all ...

Thank you for this wonderful day; you just refused to see me. The man who says he loves me refuses to see me because I have not been available enough for him. So as he suffers, he makes me suffer too, you won, I'm hurt, are you happy? I got up this morning confident and happy at the idea of seeing you, you show me that when it comes to you, trust is a ploy, you won't need to repeat your lesson I have perfectly learnt it, and you won't get to do this again, because I will not give you that opportunity. I was coming to you more surely than you can imagine, peacefully, but you brutally stopped me. I will not set a foot back in this business that felt simple and light to me despite appearances, and that you reveal to me to be tortured and toxic. I liked everything, it made me feel so good, but now I do not like it anymore and that, you see, that hurts. You have no idea how much harm you caused me, but I suppose it is proportional to the good you had done me before ...

Blandina also struggled in her hesitation, she was closing a door on him, but would let him open it again. They could love each other in the morning, break-up in the afternoon, make up in the evening, and start all over again the next day.

Tuesday, February 15, 2011

I can't read your emails at the moment, I'm not alone and I am pretending to be on my novel. I think the first time I wrote you I told you that all my (illusory) certainties had shattered, if only I knew how right I was. This one-week break might draw you away from me, the thought of it makes me sad, but there isn't much I can do about it. So, as my mother often tells me, "hope for the best, but expect the worst" I don't see the point in expecting the worst, especially since I believe that fear acts like a magnet and brings to us the things we dread. Tonight I'm puzzled and, I must say, very depressed also, I wonder what you expect from me. I look at the roses you sent, I find them so beautiful, but why are you so unfair to me? If you mute the sound, and keep only the images, things are moving forward for us, and it looks like you don't see it. Here's an image you're missing: I've been drinking a lot of wine lately, much more wine, much too much, probably so I could think less. You arrived in my life without a warning, it is clear that there was a place to fill, but why do not you understand that I must get used to this idea. In the beginning, about an eternity ago, you would tell me not to rush, because you feared that I was mistaken; and then when you say that I decide everything, it's false, when you're not available, on the weekends and Wednesdays mainly, I don't get to decide anything, so why do you not take into account those days that leave me with no option? No, you really are not fair with me. Tell me clearly what you hope for and expect from me and we will see what I will do ... I don't know if I miss you, but I think of you infinitely. And when I think of our stolen moments, their heat invades me and I feel so much better, you kiss me, you caress me, and I imagine the rest. There is always the moment when you penetrate me and that's when I lose my mind ... Do I have to be unfaithful to him before I can leave him? And if this situation "suits me" as you say, why don't you do something so that it doesn't suit me anymore?

They were deep into the "Follow me I'll flee, flee me I'll follow." Thus, when John evaded her request, she would become more, much more demonstrative ...

Friday, February 18, 2011
   You left your scent on the scarf and last night, we were invited and you were with me throughout the evening, we came home late, I got up late, and I'm about to pack my bag to leave. As I told you, I won't be taking my phone, I'm sure you understand. When I get back you'll be

gone, but I'll probably send you emails that you'll read when you return I'm not going to bother you with text messages because I know that it gets annoying when you're out skiing, and the gloves don't help ... After we parted, I regretted not having put your hand in my panties, you would have dipped your fingers and tasted how much you turn me on ... I wish you a great holiday with those you love.

I send you days and days of love ...

Saturday, February 19
I long for you.

Monday, February 21
I no longer fear,
being unhappy,
nor making a bad decision,
nor failing to make things work between us,
I know my deepest dream,
the one I have had since little,
I dream of an extraordinary Love story and I will fight for it.

A story of absolute Love,
more powerful and stronger than anything you can imagine,
a Love without doubt, untainted,
that nothing can damage and that shines like a sun,
a Love like great art,
an unconditional Love.
I do not know if it's with you that it will happen,
but I will not settle for anything else, I send you a kiss.

Doubt and questioning

Evidently, it was because she was going through a period of doubt that John had been able to enter her life so easily. Where was she at in her relationship? Her partner, Stephen, hadn't change, yet she was feeling like she was only just "discovering" his flaws.

What was her main reproach concerning him?

Probably his obstinacy in never asking himself questions, his refusal to think, and how impossible it was for them to communicate intellectually. She could see him accumulate errors, without ever wondering why. He would only note what was happening to him, without ever giving the impression of being able to change anything. Since John had confessed his Love to her, and touched her heart, she was trying to warn Stephen, but it was a waste of time. She had even heard him say that if she dumped him, it would be normal considering all the failures he accumulated. She felt about to surrender, she had the feeling she was the only one fighting, for her couple, for her day-to-day life, to keep making plans. He had told her, an eternity ago now, he wanted to get married, she had said yes, and then nothing. It is true that in everyday life, Stephen was a doll, and that everyday life takes a lot of space, but she felt an intellectual and spiritual poverty in which she started doubting she could ever blossom. She felt like she wasn't sharing anything with him anymore. He never made decisions, and it weighed on her. If she was to leave him, it wouldn't be for John. She would leave him to find herself alone again, something she deeply loved.

To love "solitude" was often badly perceived. The two years she had spent more or less single before meeting Stephen, when she dared to say that she was enjoying her single life, she could tell people didn't believe her. And yet, God knew that it was true. She would get so many invitations to go out that she had to fake having plans so she could spend a quiet evening at home. With her dog and her cat, she'd spent the night watching a romantic comedy. She loved those evenings, where it seems like nothing could come disturb her peace. If she had the misfortune of telling the truth, her entourage felt invested with the mission to, above all things, not leave her alone, because surely, it meant she was depressed.

Stephen's presence was not really oppressive, but since she was with him, she thought she had to respect certain rules, such as not making Love with another man. The problem was that she no longer wanted to make Love with him, and that her senses erupted when she thought of John or saw him, and even when she was in the presence of her friend Bandit, the big-hearted biker. Bandit had helped her get a pretty large sum of money back from an unscrupulous "friend" who thought he wouldn't have to pay her back. Stephen had not deemed it necessary to intervene, and Blandina had been very disappointed.

This event had brought her closer to the biker.

Bandit was a former mercenary who now restored old motorcycles, mainly Harley Davidsons. He had complicated and unhappy relationships, and was always in need of affection and tenderness. She would go visit him from time to time, she enjoyed talking with him, and he thought he was in love with her. Bandit would fall in love with all the pretty women who listened to him. Nevertheless, if she had not been in a relationship, she would have happily spent one night with him. "A Night of Love" as he called it, and that was it, nothing less, nothing more.

She wondered whether she was made to be in a relationship, because she loved men in general and always felt a little deprived to have only one lover. It was morals more than Love that drove her to settle down, but was it good for her? She had always thought that two beings who made Love weren't doing anything wrong, provided they were free from any commitment. Kissing, caressing, loving each other, it could not be wrong. When she would see Bandit, she could feel his infinite need for tenderness, and she wanted to give him some, for him, for her …

Being in a relationship, she abstained from it. Faithfulness in a couple seemed essential to her, but she did not really know why. Very few couples around her managed to comply with this rule, yet they all demanded it. She herself, when she was very in love with Stephen, would have been torn to find out that he had made Love with another woman. But if we really loved someone, why did we not tolerate him making Love to someone else? She had always asked herself this question without ever finding the answer. Today, it would have almost been convenient for her if he had a mistress, that way she would allow herself a lover, or two …

Can one love two men at the same time? She still loved him, but she felt that she was also in love with John. He attracted her like a magnet, but was it purely physical? She could not sort through her emotions. Despite all that was happening, or not happening rather, with Stephen, she was feeling serene by her side, she had absolute trust in him, he always made her laugh, and that was gold. And despite his repeated failures, she still had admiration for him. And she still found him so attractive, especially naked.

And suddenly ...

She had to be sure!

She suddenly decided, out of the blue, to make love with John. And so, in the middle of the afternoon, she sent him this message:

"Still eager to make love with me, Pastor?"

"Do I really need to answer this question?"

Her answer was a little long in coming, and John being the pessimistic that he was began to fear a new joke from Blandina.

The answer came:

" Where you want, when you want. "

John thought he was going to faint ... Holy cow! He did not expect that! John could hardly believe what was happening. He repeated aloud what she had just sent: "Where you want, when you want ..."

He asked her to meet him in a hotel, it was not very original, but it was a four-star hotel, and as she arrived, Blandina said it was silly to rent such a beautiful room, for so little time ... They kissed, undressed, and she laid down naked on the bed.

She was so beautiful, so sensual, he laid down on her, he caressed her, kissed her, finally he could embrace her passionately, he drank in her scent, Blandina surrendered totally in his arms, and then, looking at him in the eyes said, "Penetrate me ..."

But... he couldn't get hard.

For months now he had been hoping for that moment, now that it was happening, that she was offering herself to him unconditionally, without any restraint, he could not make love to her!

Blandina embraced him affectionately.

John, on his side, preferred not to think anymore, but his dismay was immense.

They parted, as they had met, with tenderness and with a smile.

The experience, far from having calmed Blandina, had strongly increased her desire for him, or for sex, she did not know too much. All she knew was that when she left this damn hotel she felt like she had her ass up in her head! When she arrived home, Stephen was there. She threw herself on him, and they gave in to a good fuck which pleased them both.

But the damage was done, and John imperceptibly began to grow bitter.

Lord, all those things they had written to each other, their relationship was mainly epistolary — if we can use such a word for emails — but subconsciously, unable to assume his "malfunction" he started lying about until reaching a breaking point. Today, he was remembering all his sufferings with delight, for she was now with him, at last. He still had her last emails in mind, back when he thought he was done for ...

Disappointment

Blandina was quick-tempered and would easily get carried away.

On that day, she had hung up on him again. For some time now, since this afternoon at the hotel in fact, she was left hungry for more whenever she spoke with him. She didn't settle for approximation and as she pushed him further and further in his arguments, she became to feel disappointed with his analyses.

She opened up to him by email:

I often ask for your opinion, but what I expect from you is a real reflection from your heart and I hardly ever get it. You are so "indoctrinated" that you can't trust your own ideas, what I also call your perception. It seems like you censor yourself, because you have been told that you were born imperfect and sinful and that others know better than you and have known long before you, what "is" and what "is not!" Therefore, there is no room for reflection and even less for imagination.

The result is that you often miss the point. Since you told me that you felt the Holy Spirit coming down on you, why do not you let it blossom in you in all "freedom?" Sometimes I wonder why I ask you. I thought that everything you had read and studied had greatly opened your mind and I have the very unpleasant feeling that it's the opposite; so when I tell you that you disappoint me and that I'm exploding, I'm disappointed in myself, for expecting from you what you seem unable to give me ... new ideas.

I send you a kiss.

By writing this email, she had formulated what she had been feeling for quite some time already, this sentence she had written: "you can't trust your own ideas" set her thinking, she took one of his texts in which he brilliantly argued on the question of true Love, typed the first sentence on her computer, and with tears in her eyes, she saw the whole text of her beloved Pastor appear on her screen.

Her Pastor, whose words she literally drank, whose advice she constantly sought, this man whom she believed to be very wise, had written nothing, and worse, he was incapable of thinking for himself. He had copied everything. Just changing some of the first names to make the letter feel personal.

There was not a line from him …

She repeated the experiment with a magnificent poem that he claimed to have written to her, and without hope, without surprise, the poem appeared in its entirety, also copied.

Her Pastor was just an impostor. The disappointment was huge …

Immediately, she informed him of what she had just discovered, but he, instead of lying low, attacked her maliciously. He told her that she was "a pain in the ass," that the pride that characterized her would inevitably lead to her downfall, that their story had never meant anything, and that he would be grateful if she would not write to him any more. She felt all the love she had for him crack and fall apart. Blandina ceased all contact. But less than twenty-four hours has passed when he wrote her this text: "I AM HEAVY-HEARTED! "

Then, without anger, without passion, perhaps even without feeling, she answered him:

You could have dedicated a poem of Love to me, "Your navel is a round goblet which never lacks spiced wine…" I would have been touched equally, but to claim it as yours is an imposture.

And your essay on "How do we know when we love?" You did a simple copy-paste and changed the names to make it your own, an imposture again, and you quote Cocteau, do you even know what he wrote? (I'm not asking you if you've read it) and Racine, imposture always! You do not even know what you're talking about!

You're an imposter, it's not an insult, it's the appropriate way to describe you.

But worse than the imposture you see, you insulted my intelligence by believing that I would not find out.

I understand better now why every time I asked for your opinion, your answers sounded hollow and odd.

This little voice that was saying to me "Wait, wait." It's not because it was not the right time, it's because I was soon going to find out that you do not exist …

You do not even have the courage to invent yourself…

An avalanche of emails ensued.

Blandina, of course, read the many emails he wrote to her and when she read him, trying to rub her the right way and denigrating himself with talent, it made her smile, because she thought he was messing with her.

He said among other things:

"You are out of my league,"

"I wanted to reach something that is not within my reach,"

"You are better than me,"

"I belong much lower than you,"

"I could not have what I did not deserve (how awful!)"

And now, if we made one sentence from all those different one, it could spund something like:

"I'm not worthy." That's it, "Lord, I'm not worthy of you …"
"Doesn't it remind you of something?" she thought.

Of course the wonderful poem probably expressed perfectly what he felt, but why pretend it was his? And especially when, for a long time she had asked him to answer her questions about Love. He just copied texts written by others, he could not make her believe that all the words he had copied were a perfect rendition of his feelings. The feelings and experiences of others were never ours. She sincerely thought that he had been told so many times to forget what he thought he knew that it had effectively happened, he had forgotten.

How can one write "I could not have what I did not deserve?" But who deserves what?

She had not read the Bible in its entirety, but she had read bits of it, and she did not see why she should have others explain to her what she understood, which was evolving with the years anyway.

When Jesus said, "what you do to the least of these, you do to me," what she understood was that the universe is a whole, that everything is connected, absolutely everything. So when psychology mentioned "listening to oneself, trusting one's feelings, messages from the unconscious," Blandina understood that psychology revealed the language of the soul. When science, through quantum physics, claimed that all solid and immobile matter was composed of incessantly moving particles she understood that two contradictory truths could coexist, so there was not a truth, but many truths. There were not people in the wrong and people in the right, and so those who believed in Jesus Christ, were as much in the truth as those who believed in Krishna, Buddha or psychoanalysis. The only universal truth is Love. The truth was only a question of point of view, of perspective.

And if we were made "in the image of God" then we could only be perfect, only we had forgotten we were. Why? That she did not know, but she was hoping to find out one day.

She had asked John once, why when he was a child, when he felt neither bad nor imperfect, he had let others make him believe he was? So much so that he would not even feel able to write about Love anymore.

He found her arrogant in her pursuit to write a bestseller, and he had told her "watch out for the fall."

"If I fail miserably, it will not be because of my arrogance, but because I will not have put my whole faith, my whole soul into it ..." Didn't Jesus say that faith could move mountains? So if we could move mountains with faith, we could write a bestseller too! All these passages of the Bible, she quoted them because she "felt" them, but there were some that she did not feel, and she told herself that there had to be something for everyone, that's why the Bible was so dense. But the Bible was far from being her only source of inspiration. When Didier van Cauwelaert wrote in his book Cloning Christ "If thought is a particular form of energy, love is its most powerful expression," she felt it fully, and it echoed in her mind with "faith moving mountains."

She kept all her thoughts to herself because she did not want to write to him anymore.

She answered him one last time:

It may be time for you, Pastor, to open up to other sources of information. But remember what I've already told you, you're as capable as anyone of having new ideas that do good. Now, no need to leave me messages, to send me texts or emails, I'll erase them immediately.

John tried to reach her again, but this time it was a wasted effort.

From then on, John left Blandina's life entirely. Disappointment is worse than betrayal because there is nothing to forgive, hence nothing to fix.

When a person disappoints you, it is because you discover that you do not know them, and as a result, any invested feeling becomes fake.

John knew that Blandina was not bluffing, he felt as alone and abandoned as an orphan and his distress was immense. He realized the sidereal emptiness of his own existence, he realized that there was nothing nor nobody he loved, she was right, he did not exist …

What he had been dreading from the beginning had just happened.

He felt like he had been shot in full flight. He was in a car dealership when he had received the email on his Smartphone, and after reading it he could no longer listen to the seller.

She had discovered his impostures. She did not want to see, hear, or read him anymore.

He was annihilated, he couldn't hear a sound anymore.

All his life he had pretended, deluding himself with the idea that it was the same for everyone, and that to have the impression of being free, he had to cheat. He had just realized he was wrong. No wonder he fell in love with this woman. She was beautiful, very beautiful even, but what one felt in her presence was the intoxicating scent of freedom. She was a free spirit. She was flying away while he remained nailed to the ground, miserable, in his beautiful decor where nothing authentic happened anymore.

After his email, a very long weekend began. How was he going to go on now that he knew the taste of this woman?

Still, he had to go on. Go home, sit down at the table and have dinner, without hope of receiving a message, spend the evening, the night, without expecting anything, and begin the following day …

The hardest thing was Sunday morning when he had to "play the pastor."

He felt like "the impostor" described by Blandina. He had nothing to say to them. He wanted to talk about himself, his grief, his mistakes, his distress; talk about the pretention of believing one's deep nature can be ignored, but he could not. He was supposed to show them the right path, what a heresy! There was no "right" path, there were "different" paths for everyone, to lead a happy and generous life.

She had asked him to leave her and he did not believe he would see her again.

That Sunday, he isolated himself and he cried.

On the road

But let's go back to our dinner invitation.

While they were driving, Blandina was singing along the radio's music, and John was pleasantly surprised.

This woman he had chosen truly never stopped surprising him. He had feared that this dinner would weigh on her, but clearly she rejoiced, while he was beginning to feel like he was taking her to be slaughtered by the lions in the arena ... Because nothing indicated that the wild animals would lie at her feet and purr as they did in the legend.

He knew that Philip and Martina, convinced and practicing Protestants would try to make her give him up, attempt to make her feel guilty, even scare her with the sacred bonds of marriage against "sin," "damnation" and maybe even "hell."

But Blandina, although she was a profound believer, did not believe in hell or damnation any more than she considered "sin" which seemed to her a totally abstract notion. At that moment, he thanked the heavens for Blandina's character.

They often talked about their differences of opinion about their beliefs, and he had to admit that her arguments were sound. He envied her for evolving in such a light and optimistic spirituality.

Adam and Eve

He remembered a conversation they had had a few days before in which he explained that God gave everything to Adam and Eve, but that in return, He wanted them to prove their Love to Him through their obedience. Just when John was about to highlight the downward spirals of disobedience and non-compliance, Blandina had interrupted him: "Adam and Eve were not driven out of the Garden of Eden," and she had pursued, "how could God expect obedience from men when He loves them FREE?!?!!!...."

For her, God had given them everything, yes, but without any compensation. Universal and unconditional Love does not expect anything in return.

Blandina, being a free spirit, gave much more credit to what she felt than to what she had been taught. "Huh?" he replied, "and how do you think things went?"

John was curious to hear her story, because Blandina's stories and interpretations of spiritual matters were always very optimistic and often funny, and even though he could not agree because he was Pastor, and therefore a fervent Protestant, he always took pleasure in hearing them. As a matter of fact, she had pointed it out to him:

"You like my stories, don't you?" she asked.

"I like everything that comes from you Blandina."

"Yes, but you like my stories. You find them amusing, don't you?"

"I do."

"Do they make you happy?"

John had felt that she was going to trick him.

"What is your point?"

"Do they make you happy, yes or no? Be honest!"

"Indeed, they amuse me and bring me joy.

"What if that's what "the word of God" was? Words of joy."

"Blandina stop, it's not something to joke about!"

"Something? This is what you call Him? And why couldn't we joke with Him? If God created everything, and is the origin of everything, he necessarily created humor, but clearly he forgot to gave you some. I am certain that my stories bringing you so much joy are closer, MUCH closer, to God than your threats of damnation, your heavy and boring dogmas, and your tale of Adam and Eve, driven out of paradise after having been pushed to sin in order to then be punished! All this is lousy religious stuff!"

"Blandina, tell me your holy story instead of getting worked up."

"You're right. So here, in my opinion, is how things must have happened. There was the Garden of Eden and in this garden this beautiful tree, the tree of knowledge. God warned Adam and Eve that if they tasted it, they would then want to experience that absorbed knowledge, and that for them to do so they would have to leave the garden. Adam and Eve have probably thought a lot, but how do we know what light is if there is no darkness, how do we know we're hot if we do not know cold, how do we know we love if we are not afraid of losing this Love? In fact, Adam and Eve could have stayed in the Garden of Eden like two happy idiots, but that's not what God wanted. If God gives us the choice, to follow Him or to reject Him, He wants us to choose in full KNOWLEDGE of the cause. Do you understand? It's not an imposed choice, it's a real choice, and for that you have to experience everything and its opposite ... That's why we are on earth."

John smiled and said:

"Adam and Eve did not choose to taste the fruit of the tree of knowledge, it is the serpent, who tempted Eve."

"Oh right, the serpent! The evil one! The Devil! And what was he doing there, right in the middle of paradise? One wonders! How do you not see this contradiction? Paradise, the Garden of Eden, the Kingdom of God, where everything is absolutely perfect, but still, in all this perfection, a nasty demon, who attacks two defenseless human beings, naked like worms, and God who chases them to punish them for failing to defend themselves. Well that's one awesome God, but if you came for mercy, please come back later, because right now you see, there's none in stock!"

"But Blandina, God had warned them, they could do what they wanted except taste the fruits of this tree ... They disobeyed."

"Ha, I see, God, in spite of all his magnificence and indulgence, still has a pathological need to be obeyed, feared and adored like a vulgar little terrestrial despot!"

John had to admit that Blandina had seriously shaken his convictions, but he had preferred to believe that he was dazzled, to the point of being blinded by the passionate love he had for her. A whole spiritual life in error ... No, it was not acceptable.

Pleasures of the flesh

While he was driving and growing worried of the turn the dinner might take, Blandina had gotten closer, slipped her hand under his shirt while kissing him. He felt himself lose control and carefully pulled over on the roadside. He had barely finished his maneuver that Blandina already caressed his most intimate parts with her mouth. Carried away by the pleasure, he had no choice but to give in … God it was good! If sex led to hell, it was really unfair!

John groaned in ecstasy.

Blandina put her hair back in order and said with a knowing smile:

"Now can we expect your full collaboration, both intellectual and spiritual, Pastor?" She called him Pastor when she addressed his reason rather than his emotions.

It must be said that John's desire for Blandina was such that it made it difficult for him to concentrate. One day when he was on a business meeting to sign an important contract, she began sending him erotic texts, so hot that he had almost cut his meeting short because he could not focus. Yet there were big sums of money at stake. It was at the beginning, when they were not yet together.

The dream

That morning, Blandina sent her first text message at 8 am:
"I dreamt of you last night."
"Do you want to tell me?" he had replied.
"We were in my bed, I do not know how you got there, but you were there, naked like me."
"Tell me more."
Blandina began the story of her dream, sentence by sentence, each separated by at least five minutes, so that he had plenty of time to imagine and savor the scene. She was light years away from suspecting that he was in the middle of a meeting, and lucky for him, because if she had, she would have gone even further.
"You laid on top of me, but you were not heavy."
...
"You took my wrists in your hands and you blocked them."
...
"I wanted to say something, but you stopped me by pressing your mouth against mine."
...
"You got your tongue in and you kissed me for a long time."
...
"Sill holding my wrists tight."
...
"Then you drew with your tongue on my breasts, and you caressed them with your lips."
...
"I bent with pleasure."
...
"You pressed your sex against my belly and I felt all your strength."
...
"You slipped your knees between my thighs."

...

"Then without brutality, but without complacency you spread my legs."

...

"My back was bending more and more, I was arched like a bow."

...

"And with all the intensity of your Love for me ..."

...

"You penetrated me and I deliciously lost my mind."

It's me who's about to lose my mind, he thought, Blandina was driving him crazy, he thought he was going to come just like that, in his pants just by visualizing the scene. He finished his appointment without knowing the ins and outs, signed documents without reading them, and his interlocutors found him strange to say the least, and asked him if he felt good. Without answering he nodded.

Early evening

They arrived at the door, John rang, and it was Martina who opened.

Immediately Blandina, with a big smile, gazed deep into Martina's eyes, and calling upon her soul, while greeting her, asked her inwardly: "who are you really?" Instantly the roles were reversed, Martina felt intimidated, but also seduced. This was not what she had planned …

They thought they were meeting a pretty, light-hearted woman, who was only able to turn men's heads, with no spiritual value, easy to eliminate. But Blandina was one of those people with whom you instantly feel good and who attract you.

Their hostess was no exception to the rule. When she offered to help Blandina get rid of her things, Martina was surprised to see that she did not have any. No bag, no jacket, no pocket … It was rather singular.

She led them to the living room where Philip was waiting for them.

The latter had decided that Blandina was a witch disguised as a fairy, that he was certain to be able to unmask. He was deeply misogynist and for him women were the living symbol of sin, in relation to the Garden of Eden; let us not forget that we were in the most fundamentalist den of Protestantism. So John and Blandina were like Adam and Eve, and it was entirely Eve's fault!

Blandina, as she had done with Martina, tried to reach him beyond words and senses, but in vain. He had closed his soul a long time ago.

Locked in his certainties, he was indifferent to her attempts to reach him.

They sat in the sofas in the living room to have a drink, and Blandina chose to focus on Martina, having felt their souls close together from the first second.

Martina, without knowing it had adopted her, and Philip was disconcerted by the nascent sympathy between the two women. He wondered if his wife had not lost her head, for in the end, without being mean or discourteous, it was necessary to unmask the witch, open his friend's eyes, and put everything back in the right order.

For his part, John was even more surprised and happy to see how easily Blandina could establish a warm contact.

Philip, who was a man of reason, decided not to break this relaxed atmosphere, it would be time during the meal to get to the heart of the subject and make the witch give up. And he did not dare to admit it, but he felt good too. His friend seemed happy, and this woman, with her child-like inquiring eyes, showing no suspicion, disarmed him.

And so the evening began, light and simple.

They spoke about cinema, the two women having discovered a common taste for Pedro Almodovar, a taste discreetly confessed by the Protestant, who found it all too often scandalous. They talked about bullfighting, horses, beautiful feet and shoes. Martina liked Blandina's sandals a lot.

The supper

Then they sat at the table.

John wanted to get closer to Blandina, but she sat in front of him on purpose, to avoid any excess that could have been awkward, although she thought to have anticipated them in the car when they were on their way... In public she had much more restraint than him, and did not like to "make a show" as she put it, just as she did not like to witness displays of affection.

The promisingly delicious meal began.

Blandina started eating and as she was enjoying the food, she wondered when they would decide to attack. For that is why they had invited her, and even though they seemed to like her company, she remained the tempting demon who had to be eliminated. Blandina was waiting for the court to open the meeting. But what her hosts did not know was that she had carefully prepared her argument because she had realized that the future of her love with John depended on her defense. She knew how "indoctrinated" he was. She had even heard him say many times that he loved her so much that he was ready to face "the wraths of God!"

How could one conceive of things such as "the wraths of God?"

Philip opened the meeting.

"Don't take what I am about to say the wrong way Blandina, but don't you have an issue with seeing a married man?"

"A guilty conscience?" Blandina showed him that she did not intend to avoid the subject.

"Well yes, you are breaking a couple."

Blandina could not help but smile.

"I do not think I have that power," she replied.

Philip attacked:

"But that's what you're doing! You are a believer, aren't you? Don't you fear that you will have to answer to God for your actions?"

John wanted to intervene, she was not alone in this affair, but Blandina answered before he had time to do it, very calmly, looking Philip straight in the eyes:

"Why should I fear God?"

Philip did not expect this comeback. Nevertheless, he did not lose countenance and without answering her question attacked her again. He reminded her of the commandments, the deadly sins, especially that of the flesh, he quoted some passages from the Bible telling the wrath of God, used the word "fornication" and ended with the devil and the flames of hell.

Blandina listened to him politely, but was not at all impressed; she was even disappointed at this somewhat puerile statement of the future of the soul according to the Protestants. She would have liked a subtler opponent. She answered him very sincerely.

"I do not wish to displease you more than I already displease you, but I do not share any of your beliefs except that of a single God. I do not believe in hell and even less in purgatory, I believe we all come from God and we will all return to him, without exception. If there is a hell it is here on earth. I do not believe in a God who would judge us and then punish us. I believe that our primary mission is to be happy, to find pleasure in this wonderful gift that is life…" The word "pleasure" sounded to Philip like a blasphemy. "…and that you need to have a lot of Love for yourself if you want to be able to give some to others, because we can not give what we do not have, can we?" said Blandina.

Philip intervened:

"If there is no hell, no judgment, no condemnation, then it's too easy, we can do whatever we want."

"Indeed, that's what I believe," said Blandina. We can do whatever we want. Didn't God give us free will? Of what use would this free will be if we were punished for making bad choices? I do not think I do more evil than others, although I do not feel obliged to anything. My experience of God is probably quite personal, but why should I deny it to adhere to what I am told to think?"

Philip was destabilized by these words.

"But still, to be with John although he is married, you think it's right?"

"I do not pretend to define what is right or wrong. Why don't you want to consider that John and I love each other?" As she was speaking, she took John's hand, and continued, "this man loves me and I love this man."

John thought he was about to faint; she so rarely said she loved him.

"You have no right to love him, since he is married to another woman."

Blandina felt like answering "well, in this case, he is going to un-marry," but she abstained. Philip was so judgmental, thinking only in terms of "right" or "wrong" that it seemed extremely difficult to get him out of this pattern.

Yet Blandina did not admit defeat.

"We are married until 'death do us apart', this is what you think prohibits John and I from loving each other, isn't it? Marriage was born in France in the Middle Ages, when life expectancy did not exceed 30 years, there was little time to get married more than once, even if one had wished to do so. Today we live up to a hundred years, which makes things very different. Besides, marriage was instituted for the rich and wealthy, and it was nothing more than a contract to preserve heritage. But, beyond these historical considerations, 'till death do us apart', is it not simply the death of the Love that once united us?"

Till death do us apart

Blandina reminisced…

Disappointed with her Pastor, she had dismissed him from her life, but by dismissing him, she had also driven desire out, and that was very damaging. She did not want to make Love anymore. Not at all. Her companion, who loved only her, although saddened by this state of affairs, was waiting for desire to come back to her. Stephen loved Blandina, but obviously she did not love him anymore. Only, all pretense aside, he could not live without her, quite literally. Blandina sensed that if she left him, he would die and she could not make that decision, even if, by not making the decision to leave him, it was her own life that she endangered.

"Lord, get me out of this shit!" she heard herself say more than once. Then, the destiny, or the will of the souls of John, Blandina and Stephen altogether, decided to give her a hand. In October, Stephen became ill, seriously ill. In February of the following year, five months later, he was dead. She accompanied him during these five months with all the affection and tenderness she had for him. On the eve of his death, roving between consciousness and unconscious, he said to her: "That's it, I'm setting you free again Blandina. I think I was the happiest of men by your side." He then fell into a coma, never to leave it, until his death. Blandina's grief was sincere, but leaving as he had done, Stephen was giving her the best gift there was. In addition to setting her free, he had allowed her to express to everyone, her generosity and dedication. Her availability and her courage had been praised. Blandina, supporting Stephen until his death, had become "Saint Blandina." She mourned. She had a lot of grief that she expressed without false modesty. She spent a lot of time alone, or with her animals, she let her pain go, she was finding her memories again and attempted to put them in order. Stephen had been a sweetheart to her. Never had a man been more considerate, more thoughtful, more entertaining. People reveal themselves daily with details, and it was a multitude of small details that were coming back to her. When it was cold for example and that she had to go out, he always started his car in advance so she could slip into it when it was warm. When it would rain and he was home he never forgot to open the gate so that she did not have to get out of her car in the rain, he always got up before her to make get her coffee ready for when she'd come out of the bathroom. She had stopped loving him, God knows why ... But life goes on. And Blandina, completely free, started to live again. She had been with Stephen until his death, she had died a little with him, she had cried a lot, and then she had consoled herself.

Love at last

For his part, John almost didn't think about Blandina anymore, for want of an object his desire had fallen asleep. He was no longer sending emails and had ceased to hope receiving any. He went back to work and he worked a lot, a lot more, he always left early in the morning and always returned late at night if at all, because he had a new mistress. His neighbors, Blandina's friends who rented during the winter of 2011 and had to return the house on sunny days had not come back after the summer. More than two years had passed and he had "forgotten" Blandina, he had eclipsed her. Blinded by his denial, he had so erased her from his mind that he had left his guard down…

And here it came.

He saw this woman from behind, she was wearing a light dress with thin straps. It was a very mild day. She had her hair up in a bun. He admired her neck, her tanned skin, and without realizing what he was doing he approached her… This tattoo reminded him of something… She had only just started to turn around when he realized it was her, Blandina!

Instantly, he was set ablaze with desire.

His heart was racing, his eyesight was troubled and he felt feverish.

The urge to hug her was so strong that he thought he was going to faint trying to repress it. She looked at him with that smile she had when she was embarrassed, that smile he always interpreted as mocking.

"Hello Pastor … It's been a while, hasn't it?"

She did not move, not knowing how to greet him. What he did not know was that she felt the same way he did, except that she had never tried to repress her feelings. After having mourned, she had begun to think of him again. She had realized that the deception followed by the immense disappointment that had ended their relationship had allowed her to put a clean end to her previous life. She wasn't angry with him anymore, all in all he had only sought to please her. Hoping to see him, getting ready every morning thinking of him, imagining bumping into him everywhere she went, she had been nourished by these hopes, convinced that they would not be vain. She knew her desire remained intact and was not at all surprised by what she felt.

"Yes it's been a long time."

He got closer to give her a polite kiss on the cheek, God how he desired her! How could he have ignored her, he felt so alive again! As he touched her, he felt like breathing a drug again; a drug that had done him so much good and which he had terribly, terribly missed.

John did not know that Blandina had regained her complete and total freedom and, serene that she would find him again, took advantage of this single life in which everything was allowed. She was having a lot of fun while waiting to find him again and that day had just arrived.

Blandina had preferred to let things happen on their own. She could have contacted him again, but that's not what she did. Why? Only God knows.

"You look good," he said, not knowing what else to say.

"Thank you, it's going pretty well, and you?"

"Me? I am working a lot, but I like it."

There was a pause. They were observing each other, secretly wanting each other. Blandina was waiting for him to come forward, and John thought she had grown indifferent to him. Blandina retreated.

"I have to go. See you soon?"

"Yes, see you soon."

She got into her car and left. He watched her go, regretting not having made a single move to hold her back. Now she was gone, but she had once again invaded his mind, his heart, his soul. He knew there would be no respite from then on.

She had said "see you soon," but John, an incorrigible pessimist, did not dare to hope. He went home, forgetting the two meetings he had that morning, sat down at his desk, and remained there, thinking only of her, as if all the time during which he had forbidden himself to do so came back overflowing like a tidal wave. John was seeing his whole relationship with Blandina pass before his eyes.

The day he had declared his Love, the night she first kissed him, their hidden rendezvous, their endless conversations about God, and finally that cursed afternoon she'd agreed to meet him in a hotel and where he hadn't managed to make Love to her. After that, their relationship had deteriorated. No longer feeling up to the task, he began to lie while writing to her, she had noticed and, feeling hurt, she had brutally stopped their relationship. And then, there was the scene in front of his house with his wife, he had thought he was going crazy when she had said "hello lovers" to them. After that, he had made every effort not to cross her path, even just see her, nor have any contact of any kind. He had felt an empty space that had made him suffer a lot, but, little by little, the feeling had passed, and he had imagined that he did not love her anymore, and the fact that he had a new mistress seemed to confirm just that. He was wrong. Blandina was always the one and only woman he had ever loved, the only one that provoked this burning desire, the only one that made him feel truly alive...

God knows how long he remained lost in his thoughts.

The phone rang. It was his partner.

"John? Are you okay? What are you doing? We're waiting for you!"

"Listen, I have a problem here, don't wait for me, I'll explain," he heard himself answer before he hung up.

He stayed still for a long time. Then he decided that he needed to get in touch with her, but he did not know how. He had not kept her phone number, unless ... Yes, in his old phone, he could certainly find it in the history, it had to be there. Let's hope she hadn't changed her number... He found the precious number without much difficulty.

If he called, he risked doing so at a bad time, so he sent her a text.

"You are still so beautiful..." He knew that Blandina loved compliments.

Blandina replied immediately: "Do you want to meet up?"

Of course he wanted to see her, and even more than that, he decided to call her:

"Blandina listen, how do you feel about meeting me in our new offices?"

"Of course, where is it?"

Not knowing where she was and fearing that she might be closer to the offices than he was, he said:

"Give me two minutes, I'll call you back."

He hung up, jumped into his car, and headed for his office — the new one. He did not know how their reunion was going to go, but he was sure of one thing, at that time nobody was there, and they were not likely to be disturbed. He called her back, and explained how to get to him. Then he started waiting for her. Everything had happened so quickly, she was reappearing in his life, suddenly, and was taking her place again, because nothing nor anyone could have replaced her... He was still thinking about it when he heard her park her car. He went out to greet her, and the smile she gave him revealed a lot about the pleasure she felt to be seeing him again. He put his hand on her waist, but did not kiss her on the mouth. Not that he did not dare to, but he wanted to make this pleasure last. Blandina, felt that she had to let herself go. He brought her in, showed her around the premises, and then took her back to his office. He sat in his chair, and she sat on the desk. They started talking about this and that, but Blandina devoured him with her eyes. Her desire for him was so obvious that he quickly stopped talking to kiss her.

They merged instantly. They made Love on his desk, it was the most natural thing in the world. Kisses, caresses, beautiful gestures only, and an infinite grace in their embraces ... They were made for each other, as he had told her, more than two and a half years ago... After he came, he remained a long time within her. He knew nothing of her new situation and while he had her there, he wanted to make the most of it. Both felt so good that they fell asleep for a short time. A short moment only, because the hardness of the desk surface added to the weight of John on Blandina were not really comfortable.

They separated to get up and dressed. Then John dared asking her what she was about to do.

"Now? To tell you the truth, I don't have specific plans. In fact, I'm hungry, Love whets the appetite!" It was a little after noon.

"May I invite you to lunch?"

"Here is a good idea! Absolutely!" she said happily.

"Let's go! Are you getting in my car or do you want to follow me?"

"I'm going with you."

John was a little surprised, Blandina wasn't usually so easy. She sat in his car and they left together. The desire to kidnap her, which he had had on every rare occasion when she had got into his car, cropped up again but he did not mention it.

"Still married Pastor?"

"Still with Stephen?"

"No."

John glanced at her.

"Did you break up?"

"He died."

"My God Blandina, I'm sorry."

John did not know what to say, although a fervent believer, he was not at all comfortable with death, even less so given that he understood that he was profiting from this death. He managed to ask her how it had happened.

Blandina told him everything. The sudden illness, the very bad prognosis announced from the start, how fast it had evolved, her "beautiful" role, Stephen's last words, her grief, her mourning.

Until death do us apart...

We shall not be judged

Philip remained irremediably locked into his dogmatic certainties, yet, although he refused to listen, he had heard anyway, and he felt a deep agitation.

"You interpret things to make them suit you, but it's too easy, not everyone will go to heaven, because it must be deserved, and it is certainly not by committing adultery that you will get there!"

Adultery... They had so often spoken about it, before being officially together, she knew that John felt he was "at fault" vis-à-vis God, but paradoxically not vis-à-vis his wife.

"We shall not be judged on matters of adultery."

Blandina had even called him back once to resume a conversation they had had shortly before in which he had explained his religious convictions. She had enjoyed this conversation very much, being a Catholic herself. A fervent believer, although she had not practiced for many years, she suffered at the time from a lack of spirituality around her. She had selected within her religion what corresponded to her, and had chosen to ignore what seemed to her to deny her own nature. And these questions of adultery, marriage for life, seemed to her derisory whenever she took the time to look at what was happening in the world around her. Tortures, killings, humiliations, slanders, child rapes, environmental degradation ... So, "my lover" or "not my lover," who sleeps with whom — if those were the only problems on earth, we would have been close to paradise.

She believed in a profoundly good God, loving men unconditionally, who had given her life, not a punishment! For her, people had to do everything to be happy, because since we can't give what we do not have, we must have happiness for ourselves in order to give it to others. And how could one be happy by continually upsetting one's own nature?

John the Protestant Pastor had tried to impose himself a so-called "virtuous" life in respect of the sacraments of marriage.

He had completely failed! He had had many mistresses, but the sacred appearances were safe. What a hypocrisy! What a permanent lie!

In this seemingly ideal setting, there were cracks everywhere, and he wasn't even aware of it. This beautiful house, as tidy as a show house, masked an emotional disorder that was beginning to cause serious damage. There were five of them living under the same roof, but Blandina would have challenged anyone to guess it since everything was impeccable and in order. Twice she had been invited in and she had felt the freezing cold of this soulless house.

John had had a heart attack. Blandina was teasing him, telling him that his heart, tired of beating for nothing, had almost stopped.

But the most alarming witness of all this masked mess was his own daughter who lived there. Labeled "MDD" — manic depressive psychosis — by the medical profession, this really beautiful young woman, was anorexic and suicidal. She even went as far as driving into a ravine. She had survived. This life which she had been presented with since birth was so false that only death and its definitive nature appeared trustworthy to her. Everything was so concealed, wrapped, made up, completely under control, that she could not find a way to exist. How could he not see it?

"We will not be judged on matters of adultery or sin of the flesh," Blandina was deeply convinced of it. It's lie that terrorized her. Lies were doing real damage. One only had to observe this "perfect family" in which everything was fake.

John's daughter also had a nine-year old son who lived with them when John and Blandina's affair began. Blandina felt sorry for the little boy she had never seen, because John had told him that his mother, in addition to her suicide attempts, scammed her own family, and blamed her son, telling him that she was doing this for him, because she needed money to spoil him. "What a waste!" thought Blandina.

So John and his preaching seemed so useless to her. Yes, lies had devastating consequences, and that's why she did not think she could go on with this hidden relationship, which would have appeared very innocent to ordinary mortals, since it had not yet been "consummated..."

Yet at that moment she had kept it going.

Jerome

John also had a son, Jerome. He had recently introduced him to Blandina, one day they had crossed paths. Jerome had found Blandina quite to his taste…

Jerome was the kind of boy our grandmothers would have called a rascal. He had never done much at school, did not have any degree, and was living off odd jobs and benefits. At age 35, he began to realize that money-less life is only beautiful in the movies, and that he hadn't learn how to earn a living. He harbored increasing jealousy towards all the people who possessed what he thought should be granted to him, and the first of those people was his father. He thought it was unfair not to be able to inherit his due immediately, and he was angry with him. When he met Blandina, he naturally thought that this woman should be with him, not with his father.

Although he was a handsome boy plastically speaking, since he had rather fine and regular features, he was totally devoid of charm. The jealousies and resentments he fed on a daily basis, about everything and anything, poisoned his being so much that he came across, most of the time, as someone very unfriendly, and indeed, Blandina had found him particularly unpleasant the first time she had met him.

Jerome, in addition to wanting to put Blandina in his bed, feared being dispossessed of his inheritance, because for him, it was obvious that she had seduced his father for this purpose. So he was going to seduce her, sleep with her, and throw her out like the vulgar slut that she was, and he had no doubt about the success of his endeavor.

He thought Blandina, although she was over 10 years older than him, would prefer the rejuvenated version of the father, because that's how he considered himself. He thought he was his father, better, because he was younger.

Jerome invited himself to dinner at theirs, well, at Blandina's, for John spent most of his time at her house since they had found each other again.

A first trial-like supper

From the very start of the meal he began making comments that seemed addressed to Blandina personally, punctuating them with winks and knowing grins. That made her smile, not that she was sensitive to his charm, since he did not have any, but simply because she found him more ridiculous than pathetic in his self-sufficiency. Thinking the game was won, he grew bolder:

"What does a woman like you do with an old man like my father?"

The maneuver was as delicate as an elephant would have been in a porcelain shop. Blandina wanted to laugh.

"I like everything old," she replied. Old houses, old cars, old gentlemen… The old gives everything and every being an indefinable charm I truly appreciate. Your father," she added with a motherly tone, "your father... How could I put it? I love him, that's all," she said with a broad smile.

Jerome, feeling ridiculed, was furious; he attacked her directly:

"Isn't it rather his money that you love?"

Before John had time to intervene, she burst out laughing.

"His money?" Blandina decided to mess with him, "clearly you are not very observant. Anyone in your place would have found some details revealing that I probably possess 10 times more than your father does. There is what I earn, what I have inherited from my father, and what is yet to come."

Of course she was bluffing, but Jerome did not know it. He looked at the jewels she was wearing and noticed, a little late, the two diamonds she had. One on the finger and one around the neck…

There were big diamonds, so big that he wondered whether they were real, but from what she had just said, they had to be.

She continued:

"And then you seem to forget something, it's my home in which your father lives, and I don't remember asking him for a rent; but I'll have to think about it," she joked, "right darling? Because if I don't take advantage of your money, it's not fair that you should take advantage of mine."

Jerome felt pathetic and that's what he was: a pathetic man.

Blandina rubbed it in:

"If you are waiting to inherit from your father so that your life takes off, unless an accident occurs, it is likely that you will inherit after you are 80! It will probably feel like a long wait..."

Jerome did not know what to say.

Blandina was not mean and decided to throw him a bone. Plus, a wounded animal in the wild always threatened to become dangerous.

"Of course I'm kidding, I know that you are not waiting to inherit from you father, just like I know that you don't really think I am with him for his money..."

Grateful to be able to save face, he replied:

"No, of course, I was joking too."

John had not opened his mouth, partly because he was stupefied by his son's effrontery, and secondly because Blandina's repartee always left him admiring and voiceless. Anyway, no one was fooled about what had happened, Blandina had put Jerome back in his place without any difficulty, she had "snubbed" him like the (35 years) young brat that he was, but even if no one was fooled, everyone could believe that others were, which avoided resentment, rancor, and other poisons of existence. Blandina had impressed Jerome, and it was clear now that he would no longer allow himself to behave in a way that was akin to disrespect.

The conversation resumed on a more light-hearted note and Jerome ceased his seduction game. He no longer looked at Blandina as an object of lust, he forgot his shady intentions, and for the first time in a long time, he let himself go to simply appreciate the moment without being in competition with his father. He agreed to consider Blandina as his "mother-in-law," he joked, laughed at the jokes, and stopped taking himself seriously. John perceived this change, he found his little boy for whom he had so much Love and tenderness again, and he could not remember how long ago he had felt that way. This meal had just entered moments of eternity, those parentheses in life that seem to contain all the tenderness of the world.

Such was the magic power of Blandina.

Back to the supper

John spoke up this time:

"If someone is committing adultery here it's me, Blandina is not married.

"Perhaps, but it's because of her," replied Philip.

At that moment, Blandina decided that this conversation had lasted long enough. She got up and got closer to John, grabbed both his hands and making a funny face, she said in a deep and resounding voice:

"It's me Lilith rising from hell for your eternal damnation!"

The grimace she had just made was so funny that John and Martina burst out laughing, and were thankful to her for having relaxed the atmosphere, which was getting heavier by the minute. But Philip had never heard of Lilith — Adam's first wife and the first demon according to legend — and he did not want to laugh at all.

"There's nothing to laugh about."

"Really?" Said Blandina. "It is interesting to note the common denominator linking all fundamentalists of all religions."

Without paying attention to the fact that she had just called him a fundamentalist, he asked:

"And what is this common denominator?"

"Fear. According to you, the path that should lead us to universal and unconditional Love is fear.

There was nothing left to add, Blandina had just closed the debate.

She took her glass, raised it towards Philip and with a smile, she asked innocently:

"Friend or enemy?"

Philip, despite his certainties, despite his misogyny, despite everything, was a good man and did not want to offend his friend John, so he gave a big smile to Blandina and replied:

"Friend."

Phew! Everyone breathed. Because loving is so much easier…

The evening continued in good spirits, and Philip and Martina forgot about the reason why they had invited her.

Such was the magic power of Blandina.

After supper

After John and Blandina had left, Philip and Martina felt like two idiots.

They began to tidy up and clean without talking to each other, without looking at each other. It seemed like they wanted to leave no trace of that dinner, as if it were a crime scene. They had completely broken the promise they hade made to John's wife. Not only did they have a great evening with a "sinful" couple, but they had also wished to see them again soon.

John's wife, the scorned, deceived, abandoned, desperate woman who was as much their friend as John, had implored them on behalf of 25 years of friendship, and 35 years of marriage, to help her get her husband back.

Philip and Martina felt so guilty.

They had loved Blandina. They had laughed, laughed a lot in her company, and now that she had left with John, they were mad at themselves because they knew the distress of his wife. They knew she was waiting for their phone call, "even if it's late," she had said. What could they tell her?

Besides, they envied John. No longer in love with each other, they lived in quiet boredom for never having dared to break the rules of marriage imposed by their religion. Philip had almost sinned years before, but someone from this charming Protestant community had simply snitched on him as a good rectifier of wrongs. He had had to confess in public, like Bill Clinton for Monica's blowjob. His wife, then landing the most beautiful role of her existence, that of the deceived woman who forgives for Love, was awarded with the everyone's compassion. Her husband ashamed and regretful, was even grateful to her. It was not very rock 'n' roll but it was reasonable. Of course they were not really unhappy together, but they clearly weren't exuding joie de vivre. And an evening like the one they had just had, had not happened to them for so long that they had forgotten what a pleasure it was.

"Pleasure," definitely the highway to hell! Philip decided to lie to John's wife, of course lying was a sin, but there were white lies. For the time being, it was necessary to preserve her, because she was suffering. He picked up his phone.

"Good evening Claire, they just left."

"Together? Why didn't John stay with you?"

"Listen... he had to drive her back."

"How did it go?"

"Not too bad, but you know, he is completely bewitched by her, he can't hear a word we say; be patient, it won't last, besides she drinks like a fish, he'll get tired of it."

"You didn't talk to him, did you?"

"I promise you I did, but he's so in love with her that..."

"Love" the word had slipped out, shit, it was definitely not what he should have said.

"In love? Oh no! Philip don't say that!" she burst into tears.

"Claire, stop, listen to me..."

At that moment, Martina grabbed the phone and said:

"I'm coming."

Martina took the car keys and without saying a word to Philip went to join Claire.

When she arrived, it was a little ball of misfortune who opened the door. Claire was in tears, and her sadness was heartbreaking but Martina who had spent the evening with John and Blandina, and who had found that these two loved each other in the purest and most complete way there is, decided to stop lulling her friend with the illusion that her husband was going to come back to her. She knew that John had stopped loving his wife a long time ago. He had had a lot of mistresses, and Claire had always closed her eyes to it. Ignoring problems does not make them disappear. She tenderly took her friend in her arms and began talking to her.

"You can not force him to love you, and you know he has stopped loving you a long time ago. You told me that you had not made Love in year, you said it did not really matter, but you were lying to yourself."

Claire replied,

"But that's not all there is in marriage."

"No, but that's mainly what it is. Making Love is what differentiates your husband from other men. When you tell people "here is my husband," implicitly, you inform them that you are making Love with this person. You convinced yourself that you could do without, and you hoped that he would do the same, in the name of "marriage," and look at the result, your beauty fades, and you think you're old, so what? What are you waiting for now? The end? Don't you think it's a bit early? I'm not going to lie to you, I've seen them tonight, and they're beautiful because they're happy. I know that you are suffering, but your love story is long over, and you have become attached to appearances, to what people will say, but this is about YOUR life, and in the end, married or not, you will die alone, and the only thing you will take with you are your memories, so try to make new ones, beautiful ones.

Martina took Claire's two hands, and looking at her right in the eye, said gently:

"Claire, John is not coming back."

"But I'm so scared to end up alone…"

"You have been alone for a long time, and nothing forces you to remain this way."

"But I love him, you know? I still love him."

"If you love him as much as you say, be happy that he is happy, but I do not think you still love him. You know, with hindsight, when Philip had his affair, I should have left him, not that it was unforgivable, but we didn't love each other, and by staying together, we forbid ourselves to be happy, each on our own. Of course we love each other, but like good friends. I will never have the courage to do what John did, but I envy him. Since it is him who is leaving you, take it as an opportunity to start again. You're beautiful Claire, just remember it.

Claire sighed deeply and felt soothed by her friend's words. At last the truth was being spoken, and it was so liberating. She wanted to look at herself in the mirror, but Martine stopped her.

"Not yet," she told her, "you're too ugly right now!"

They burst out laughing.

That night, John's wife slept soundly. She had stopped fighting against her pipe dreams, she had finally agreed to face the reality of her life, an essential step towards making a change. "You're beautiful Claire, just remember it." Martina's words echoed in her dreams. She was beautiful, it is true. She had green eyes glittering with gold, long black hair, such a pretty smile...

Unfortunately, few had seen her smile lately. Obviously when your husband cheats on you, you can lose your smile, but Claire had not smiled for years, or even decades... Like a flower deprived of water and light, she had faded. She had wanted to take on the role of the devoted and virtuous wife, but a role without joy nor pleasure is never a good one, because life is not a punishment.

About the Author

Lydwine van Deinse was born in 1967 in Paris, author of numerous essays and short stories. Thanks to self-publishing, she is putting one of her stories out in the world for the first time, and in doing do, introduces us to two characters entangled in their inconsistencies, who are going to have a hard time finding each other.

www.ingramcontent.com/pod-product-compliance
Lightning Source LLC
Chambersburg PA
CBHW020330130626
46549CB00003B/1113